SHOWDOWN ON THE SMUGGLER'S MOON: VOLUME 4

It is a period of renewed hope for the Rebellion. Luke Skywalker's quest to learn the ways of the Jedi brought him to the notorious Smuggler's Moon of Nar Shaddaa, where his lightsaber made him a quick target for a particularly crafty pickpocket. Soon after he found himself held prisoner by the Jedi artifact collector GRAKKUS THE HUTT.

Meanwhile, when searching the galaxy for a suitable location for the new rebel base, Princess Leia and Han Solo ran afoul of Imperial patrol ships. They took refuge on a remote planet only to find out they were not alone after all; Sana Solo – a woman who claimed to be Han's wife – made the call to turn Leia in to the Imperials.

The tables turn quickly, however, when Han reveals that he too is a rebel, and the only way Sana will get what she came for is if she saves them both....

JASON AARON   STUART IMMONEN   WADE VON GRAWBADGER   JUSTIN PONSOR
Writer   Artist   Inker   Colorist

CHRIS ELIOPOULOS   IMMONEN, VON GRAWBADGER, PONSOR   HEATHER ANTOS
Letterer   Cover Artists   Assistant Editor

JORDAN D.   C.B.   AXEL   JOE   DAN
WHITE   CEBULSKI   ALONSO   QUESADA   BUCKLEY
Editor   Executive Editor   Editor In Chief   Chief Creative Officer   Publisher

For Lucasfilm:
Creative Director MICHAEL SIGLAIN
Senior Editor FRANK PARISI
Lucasfilm Story Group RAYNE ROBERTS, PABLO HIDALGO,
LELAND CHEE

ABDO
Spotlight

ABDOPUBLISHING.COM

Reinforced library bound edition published in 2017 by Spotlight,
a division of ABDO, PO Box 398166, Minneapolis, Minnesota 55439.
Spotlight produces high-quality reinforced library bound editions for
schools and libraries. Published by agreement with Marvel Characters, Inc.

Printed in the United States of America, North Mankato, Minnesota.
092016
012017

 THIS BOOK CONTAINS
RECYCLED MATERIALS

marvelkids.com

PUBLISHER'S CATALOGING IN PUBLICATION DATA

Names: Aaron, Jason, author. I Bianchi, Simone ; Ponsor, Justin ; Immonen, Stuart ;
Von Grawbadger, Wade, illustrators.
Title: Showdown on the Smuggler's Moon / writer: Jason Aaron ; art: Simone
Bianchi ; Justin Ponsor ; Stuart Immomen ; Wade Von Grawbadger.
Description: Reinforced library bound edition. I Minneapolis, Minnesota : Spotlight,
2017. I Series: Star Wars : Showdown on the Smuggler's Moon
Summary: After reading Ben Kenobi's journal, Luke Skywalker is imprisoned during
his search for a Jedi Temple, while Han and Leia flee from some Imperial troops
with help from an unexpected foe, and Chewbacca and C-3PO are attacked by
a mysterious bounty hunter.
Identifiers: LCCN 2016941802 I ISBN 9781614795544 (volume 1) I ISBN
9781614795551 (volume 2) I ISBN 9781614795568 (volume 3) I ISBN
9781614795575 (volume 4) I ISBN 9781614795582 (volume 5) I ISBN
9781614795599 (volume 6)
Subjects: LCSH: Star Wars fiction--Comic books, strips, etc.--Juvenile fiction. I
Graphic novels--Juvenile fiction.
Classification: DDC 741.5--dc23
LC record available at https://lccn.loc.gov/2016941802

Spotlight

A Division of ABDO
abdopublishing.com

STAR WARS™

SHOWDOWN ON THE SMUGGLER'S MOON

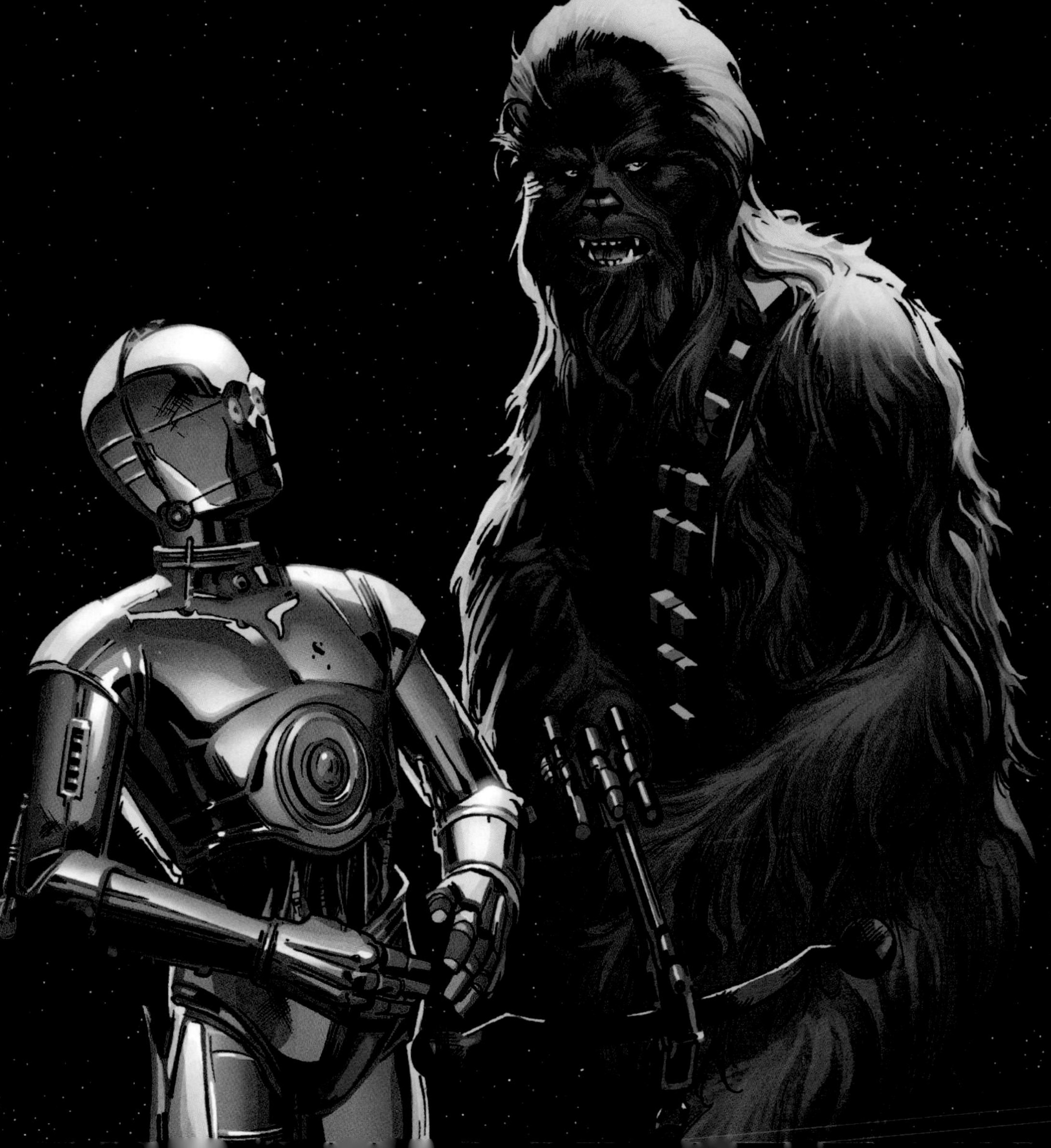

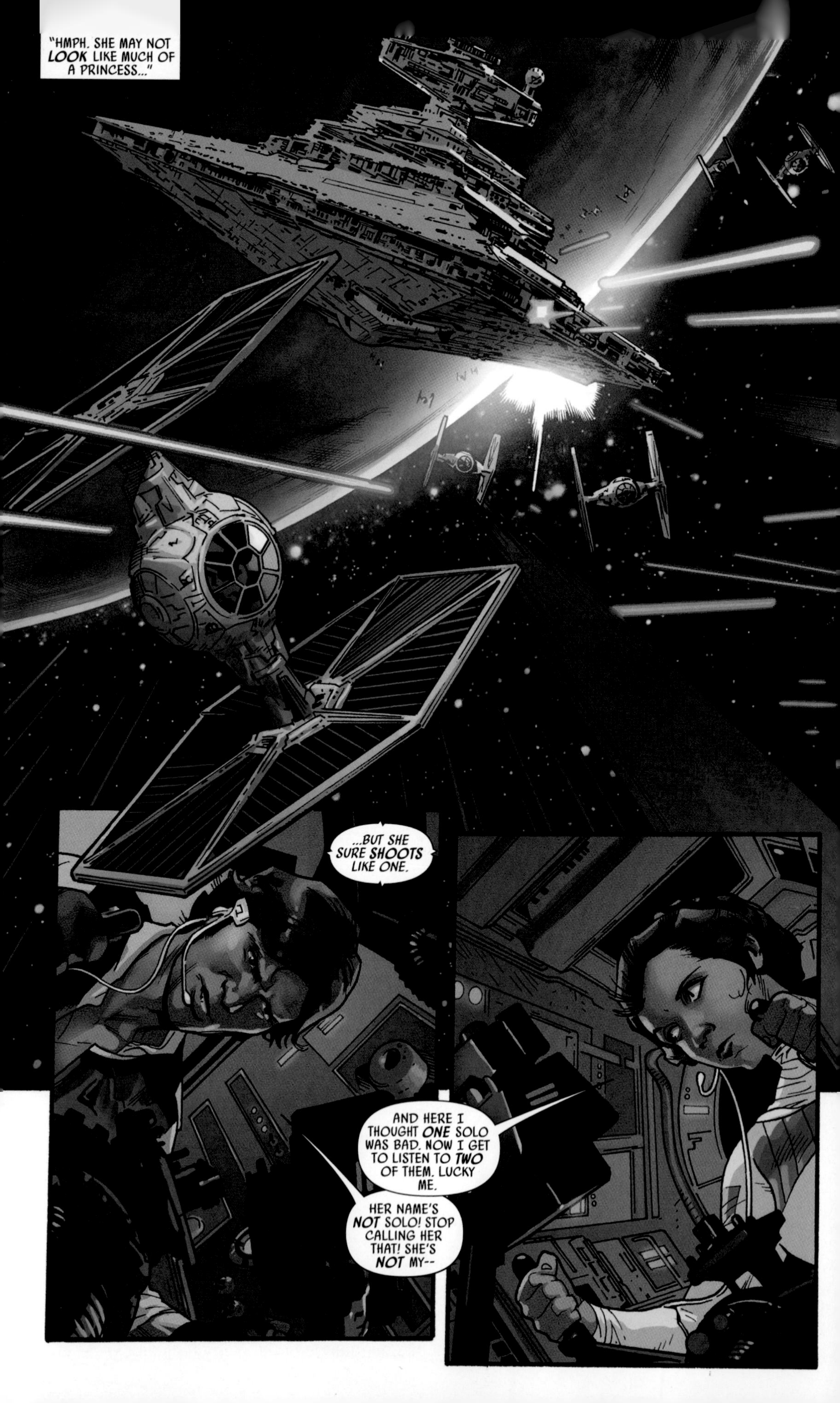
"HMPH. SHE MAY NOT LOOK LIKE MUCH OF A PRINCESS..."
...BUT SHE SURE SHOOTS LIKE ONE.
AND HERE I THOUGHT ONE SOLO WAS BAD. NOW I GET TO LISTEN TO TWO OF THEM. LUCKY ME.
HER NAME'S NOT SOLO! STOP CALLING HER THAT! SHE'S NOT MY--

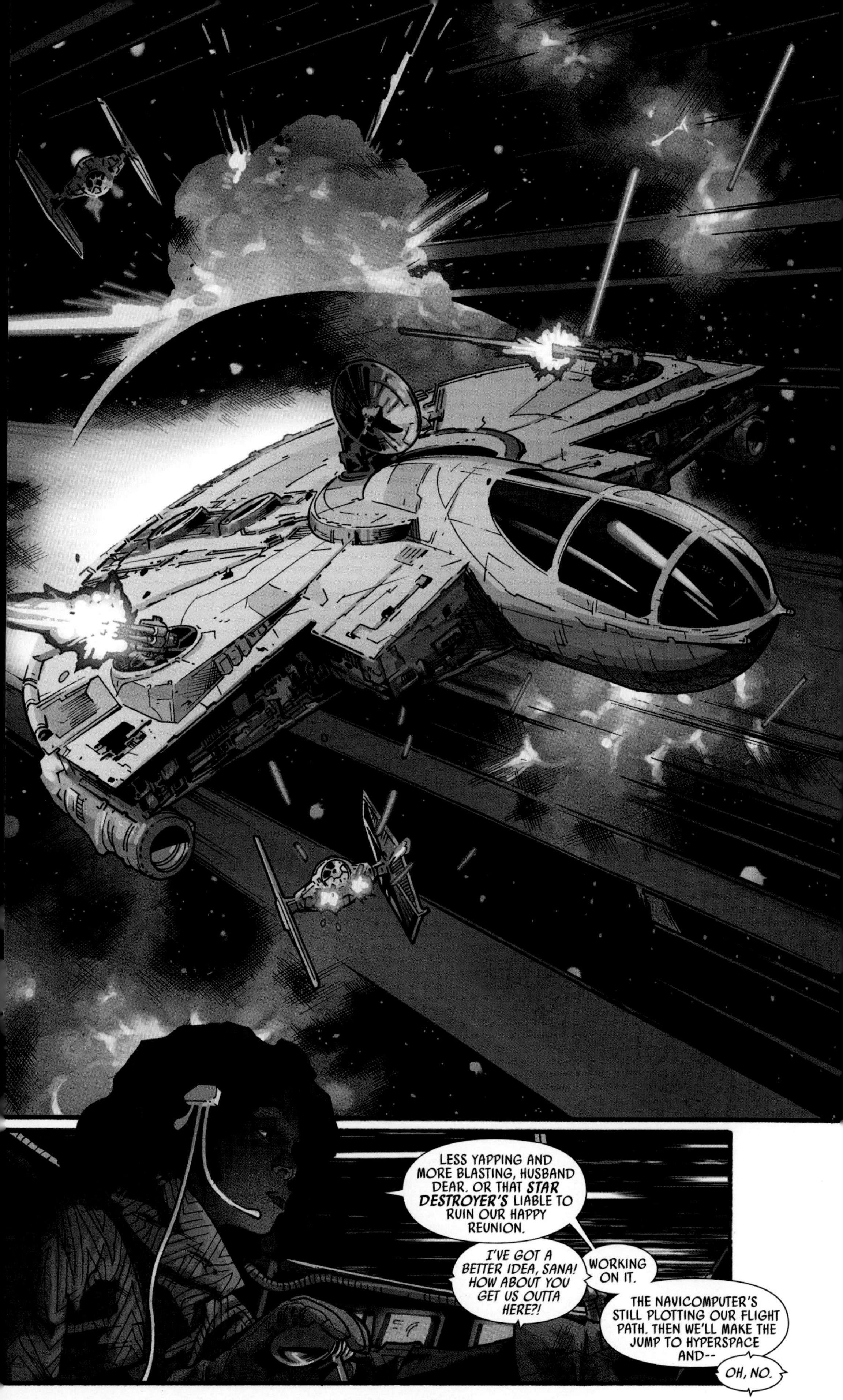
LESS YAPPING AND MORE BLASTING, HUSBAND DEAR. OR THAT STAR DESTROYER'S LIABLE TO RUIN OUR HAPPY REUNION.
I'VE GOT A BETTER IDEA, SANA! HOW ABOUT YOU GET US OUTTA HERE?!
WORKING ON IT.
THE NAVICOMPUTER'S STILL PLOTTING OUR FLIGHT PATH. THEN WE'LL MAKE THE JUMP TO HYPERSPACE AND--
OH, NO.

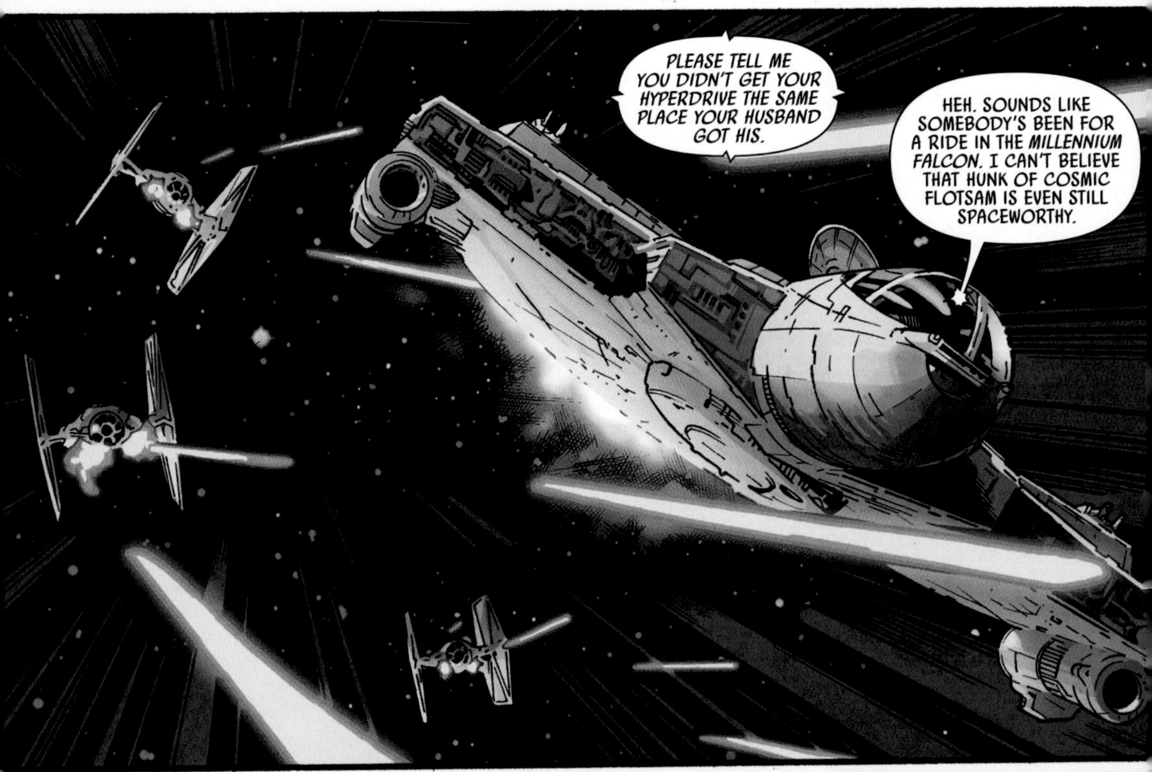
PLEASE TELL ME YOU DIDN'T GET YOUR HYPERDRIVE THE SAME PLACE YOUR HUSBAND GOT HIS.
HEH. SOUNDS LIKE SOMEBODY'S BEEN FOR A RIDE IN THE *MILLENNIUM FALCON*. I CAN'T BELIEVE THAT HUNK OF COSMIC FLOTSAM IS EVEN STILL SPACEWORTHY.

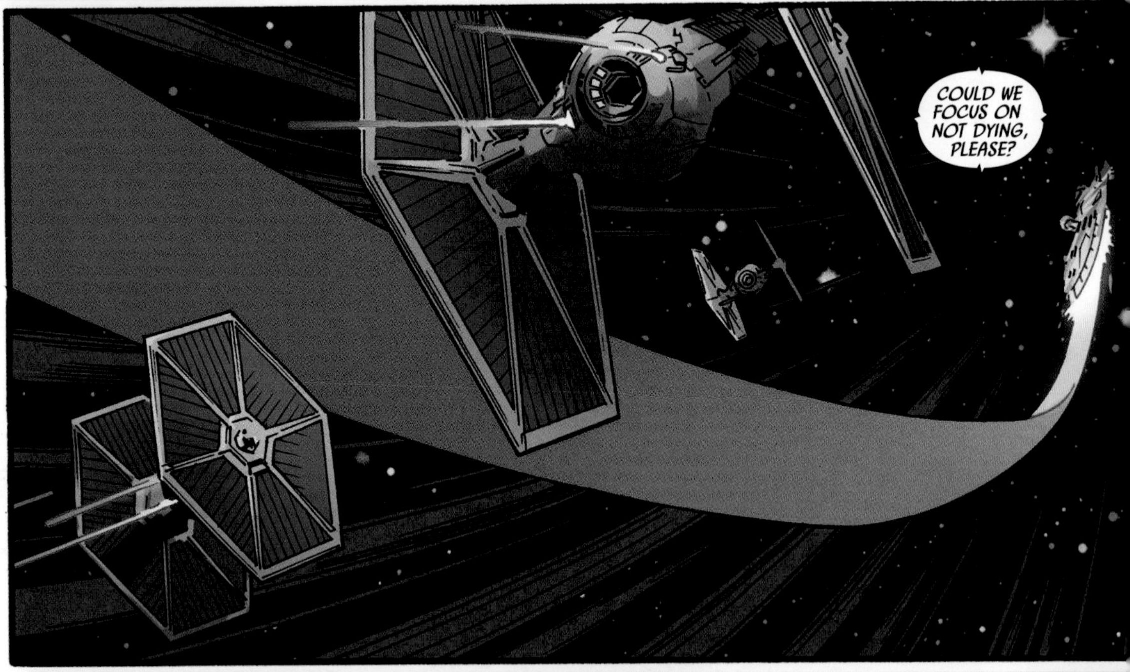
COULD WE FOCUS ON NOT DYING, PLEASE?

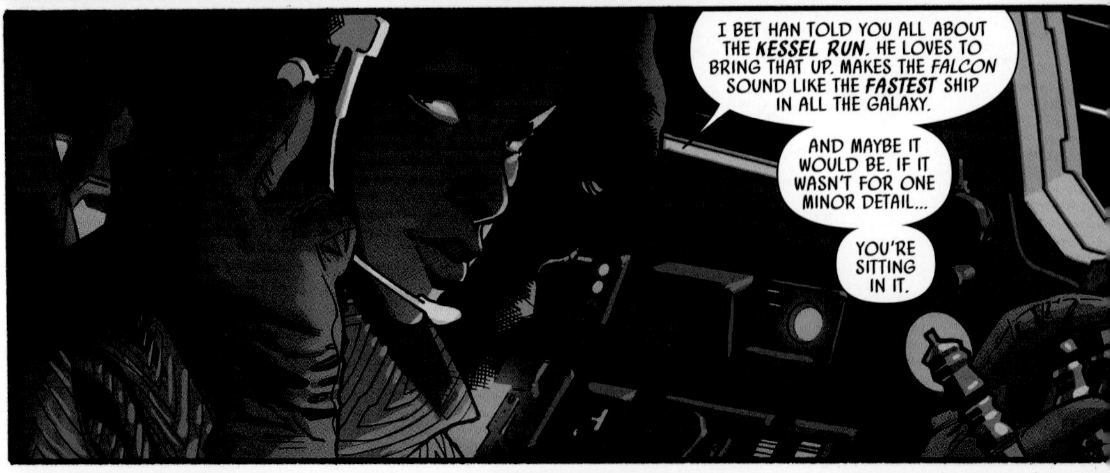
I BET HAN TOLD YOU ALL ABOUT THE ***KESSEL RUN***. HE LOVES TO BRING THAT UP. MAKES THE *FALCON* SOUND LIKE THE ***FASTEST*** SHIP IN ALL THE GALAXY.
AND MAYBE IT WOULD BE. IF IT WASN'T FOR ONE MINOR DETAIL...
YOU'RE SITTING IN IT.

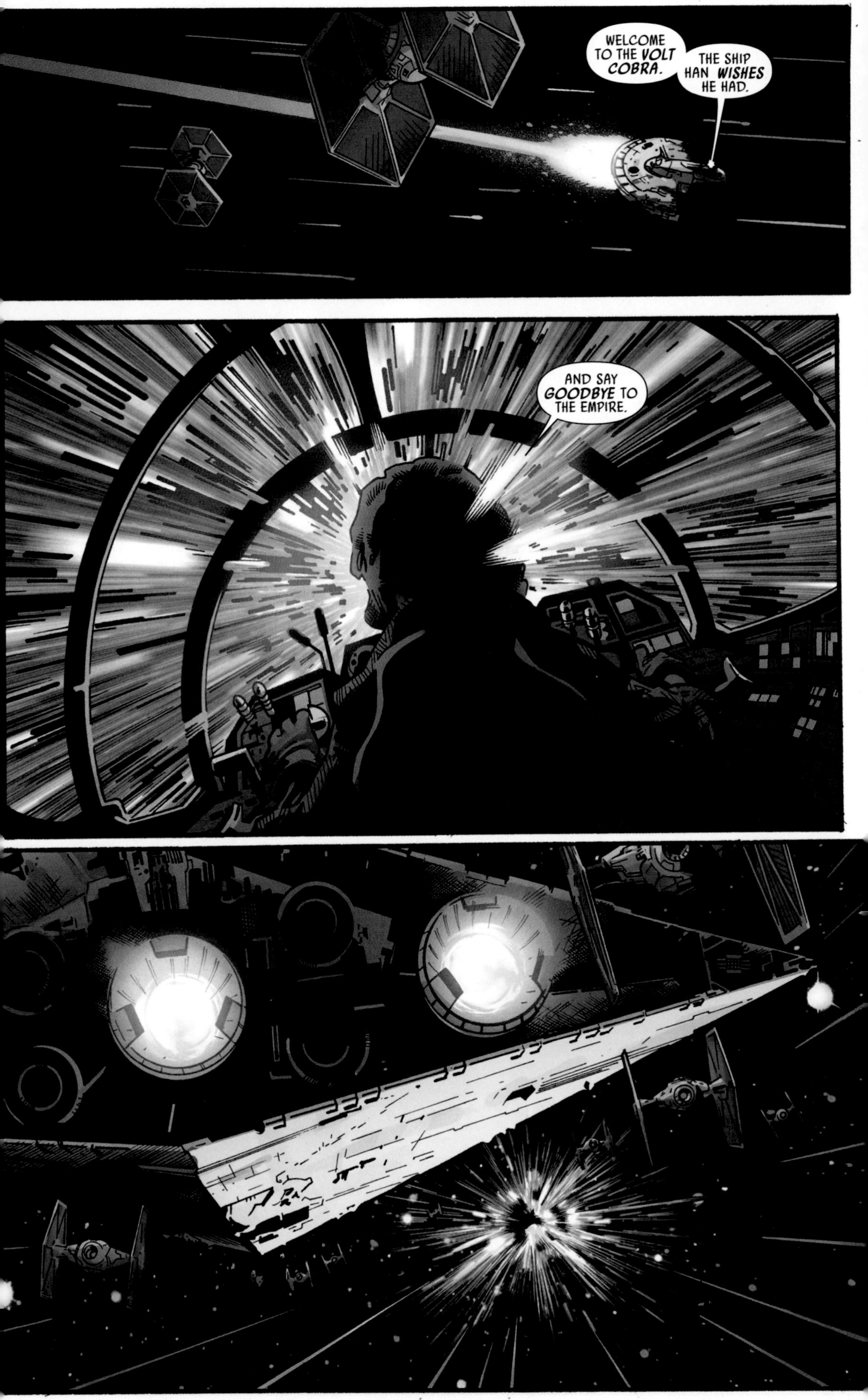
WELCOME TO THE VOLT COBRA.
THE SHIP HAN WISHES HE HAD.
AND SAY GOODBYE TO THE EMPIRE.

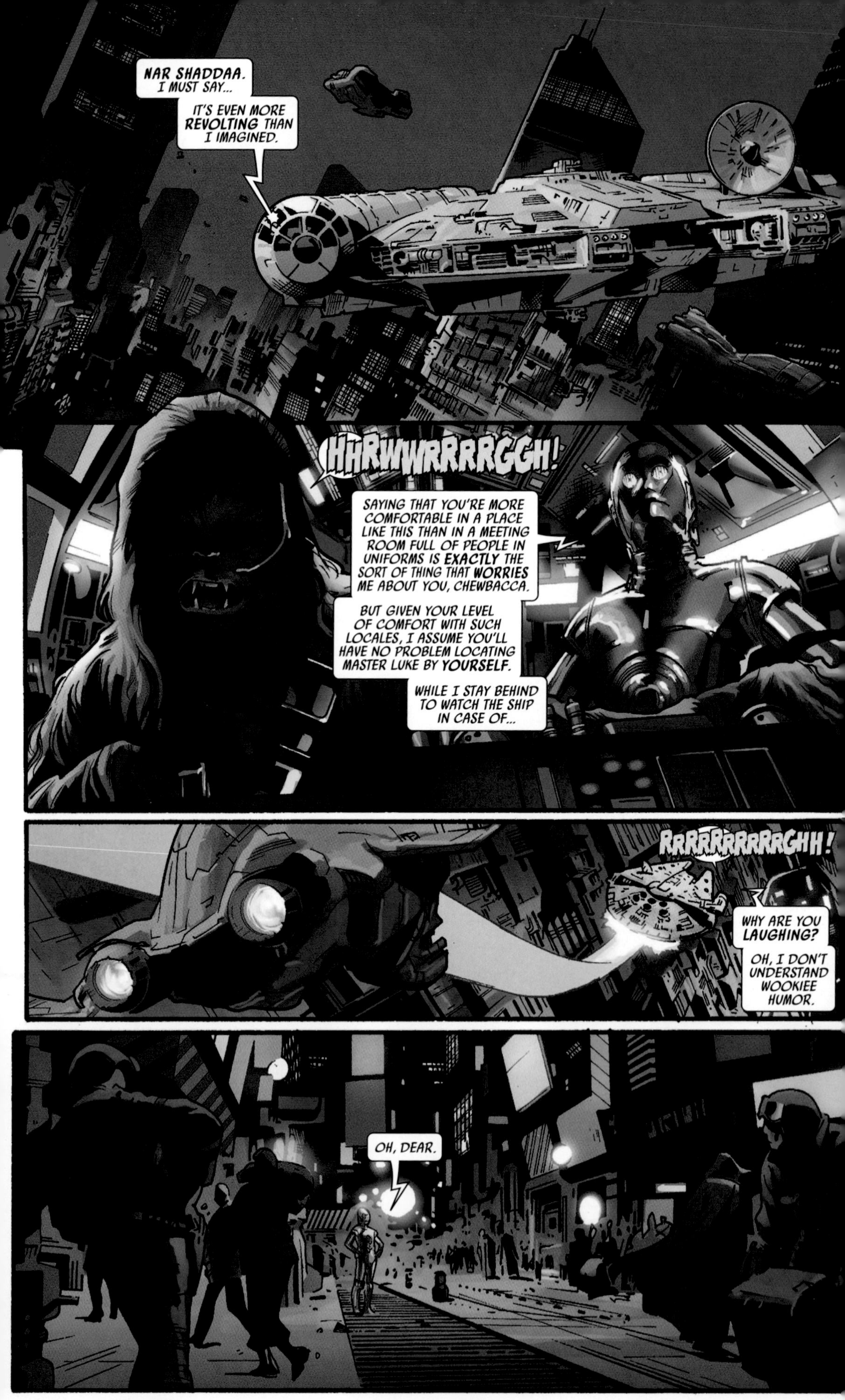
NAR SHADDAA. I MUST SAY...
IT'S EVEN MORE REVOLTING THAN I IMAGINED.
HHRWWRRRRGGH!
SAYING THAT YOU'RE MORE COMFORTABLE IN A PLACE LIKE THIS THAN IN A MEETING ROOM FULL OF PEOPLE IN UNIFORMS IS EXACTLY THE SORT OF THING THAT WORRIES ME ABOUT YOU, CHEWBACCA.
BUT GIVEN YOUR LEVEL OF COMFORT WITH SUCH LOCALES, I ASSUME YOU'LL HAVE NO PROBLEM LOCATING MASTER LUKE BY YOURSELF.
WHILE I STAY BEHIND TO WATCH THE SHIP IN CASE OF...
RRRRRRRRRRGHH!
WHY ARE YOU LAUGHING?
OH, I DON'T UNDERSTAND WOOKIEE HUMOR.
OH, DEAR.

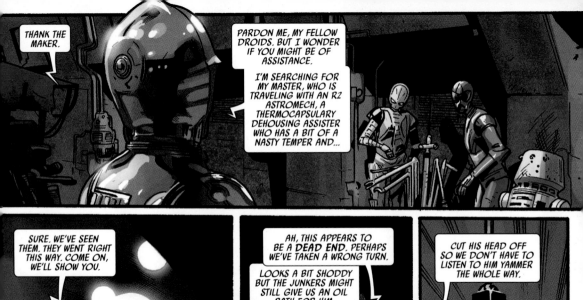

THANK THE MAKER.

PARDON ME, MY FELLOW DROIDS. BUT I WONDER IF YOU MIGHT BE OF ASSISTANCE.

I'M SEARCHING FOR MY MASTER, WHO IS TRAVELING WITH AN R2 ASTROMECH, A THERMOCAPSULARY DEHOUSING ASSISTER WHO HAS A BIT OF A NASTY TEMPER AND...

SURE. WE'VE SEEN THEM. THEY WENT RIGHT THIS WAY. COME ON, WE'LL SHOW YOU.

OH, WHAT LUCK.

AH, THIS APPEARS TO BE A DEAD END. PERHAPS WE'VE TAKEN A WRONG TURN.

LOOKS A BIT SHODDY BUT THE JUNKERS MIGHT STILL GIVE US AN OIL BATH FOR HIM.

CUT HIS HEAD OFF SO WE DON'T HAVE TO LISTEN TO HIM YAMMER THE WHOLE WAY.

THESE DROIDS SEEM TO BE NOTHING MORE THAN COMMON CRIMINALS. TRUST ME, I AM AS SHOCKED AS YOU ARE.

PERHAPS WE SHOULD TRY ASKING SOMEONE ELSE?

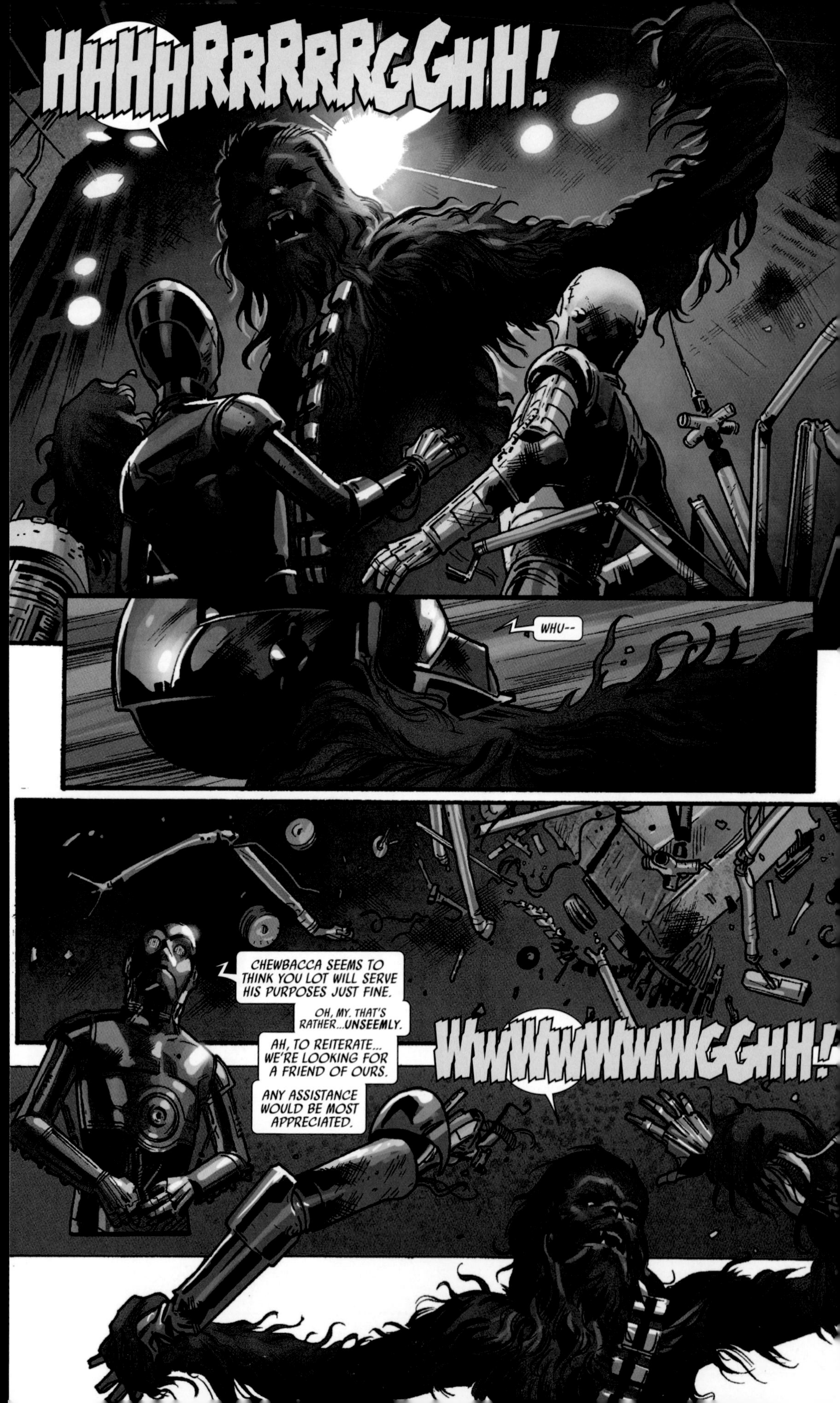
HHHHRRRRRRGGHH!
WHU--
CHEWBACCA SEEMS TO THINK YOU LOT WILL SERVE HIS PURPOSES JUST FINE.
OH, MY. THAT'S RATHER...UNSEEMLY.
AH, TO REITERATE... WE'RE LOOKING FOR A FRIEND OF OURS.
ANY ASSISTANCE WOULD BE MOST APPRECIATED.
WWWWWWWWGGHH!

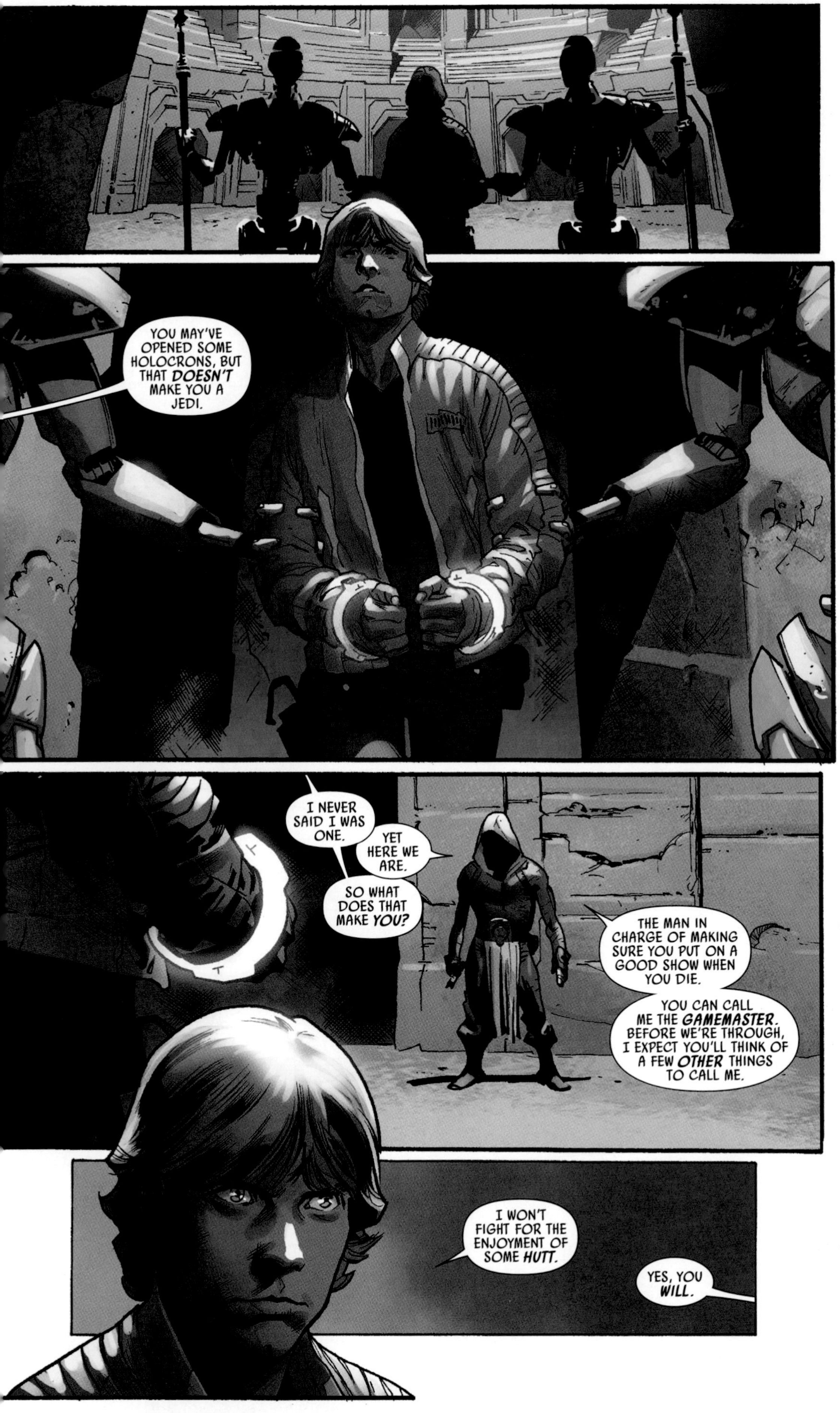
YOU MAY'VE OPENED SOME HOLOCRONS, BUT THAT DOESN'T MAKE YOU A JEDI.
I NEVER SAID I WAS ONE.
YET HERE WE ARE.
SO WHAT DOES THAT MAKE YOU?
THE MAN IN CHARGE OF MAKING SURE YOU PUT ON A GOOD SHOW WHEN YOU DIE.
YOU CAN CALL ME THE GAMEMASTER. BEFORE WE'RE THROUGH, I EXPECT YOU'LL THINK OF A FEW OTHER THINGS TO CALL ME.
I WON'T FIGHT FOR THE ENJOYMENT OF SOME HUTT.
YES, YOU WILL.

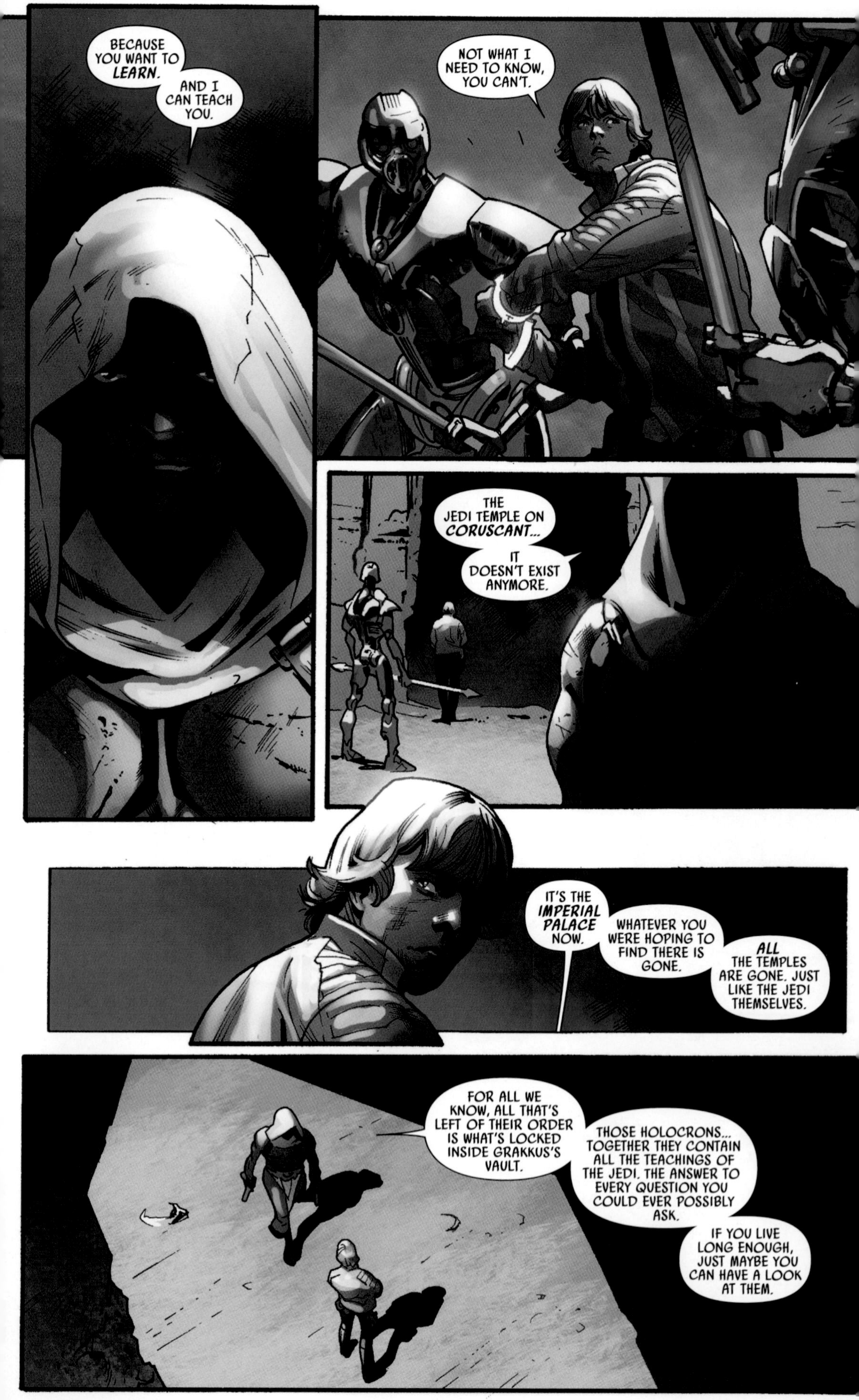
BECAUSE YOU WANT TO LEARN.
AND I CAN TEACH YOU.
NOT WHAT I NEED TO KNOW, YOU CAN'T.
THE JEDI TEMPLE ON CORUSCANT...
IT DOESN'T EXIST ANYMORE.
IT'S THE IMPERIAL PALACE NOW.
WHATEVER YOU WERE HOPING TO FIND THERE IS GONE.
ALL THE TEMPLES ARE GONE. JUST LIKE THE JEDI THEMSELVES.
FOR ALL WE KNOW, ALL THAT'S LEFT OF THEIR ORDER IS WHAT'S LOCKED INSIDE GRAKKUS'S VAULT.
THOSE HOLOCRONS... TOGETHER THEY CONTAIN ALL THE TEACHINGS OF THE JEDI. THE ANSWER TO EVERY QUESTION YOU COULD EVER POSSIBLY ASK.
IF YOU LIVE LONG ENOUGH, JUST MAYBE YOU CAN HAVE A LOOK AT THEM.

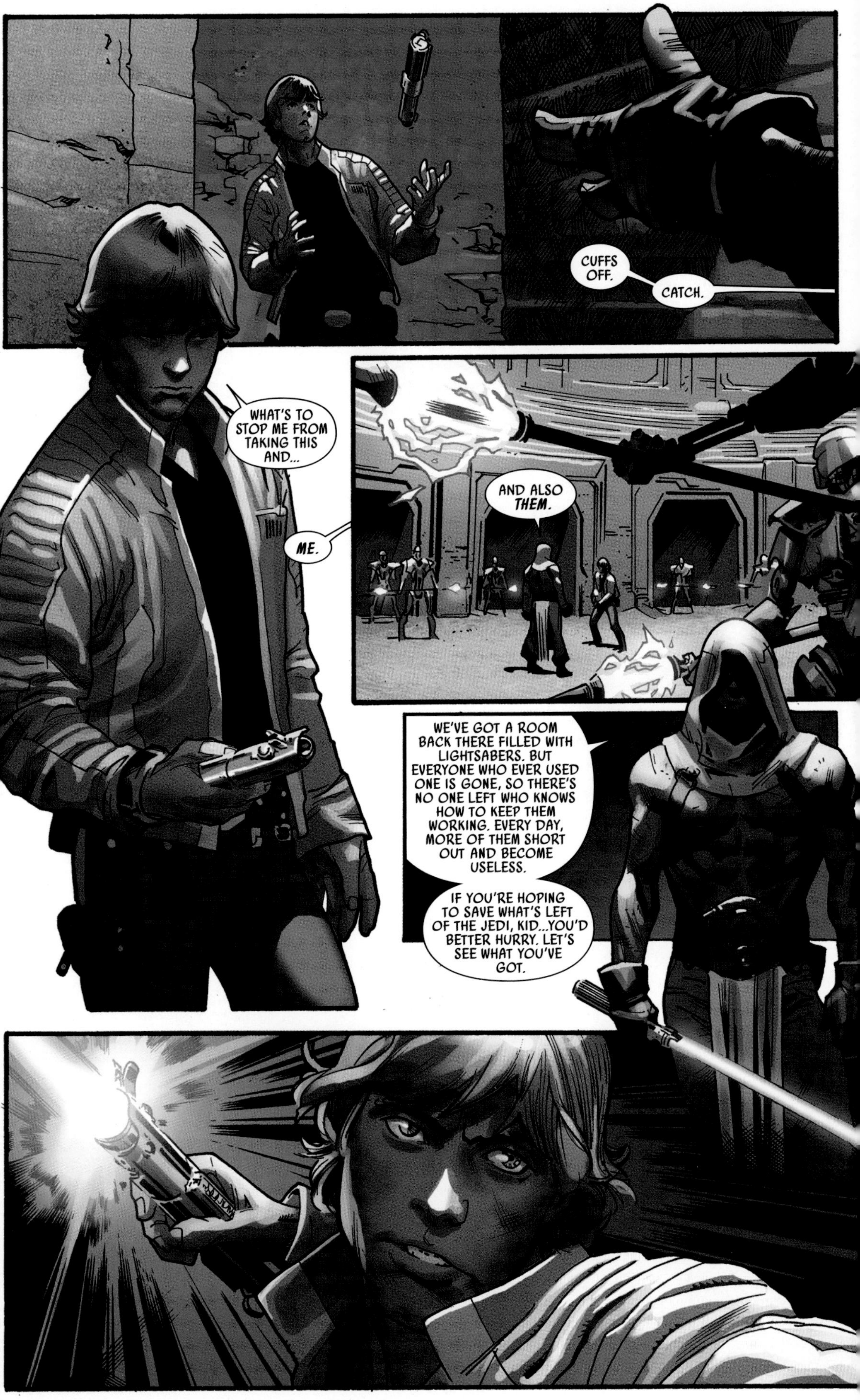
CUFFS OFF.
CATCH.
WHAT'S TO STOP ME FROM TAKING THIS AND...
ME.
AND ALSO *THEM.*
WE'VE GOT A ROOM BACK THERE FILLED WITH LIGHTSABERS. BUT EVERYONE WHO EVER USED ONE IS GONE, SO THERE'S NO ONE LEFT WHO KNOWS HOW TO KEEP THEM WORKING. EVERY DAY, MORE OF THEM SHORT OUT AND BECOME USELESS.
IF YOU'RE HOPING TO SAVE WHAT'S LEFT OF THE JEDI, KID...YOU'D BETTER HURRY. LET'S SEE WHAT YOU'VE GOT.

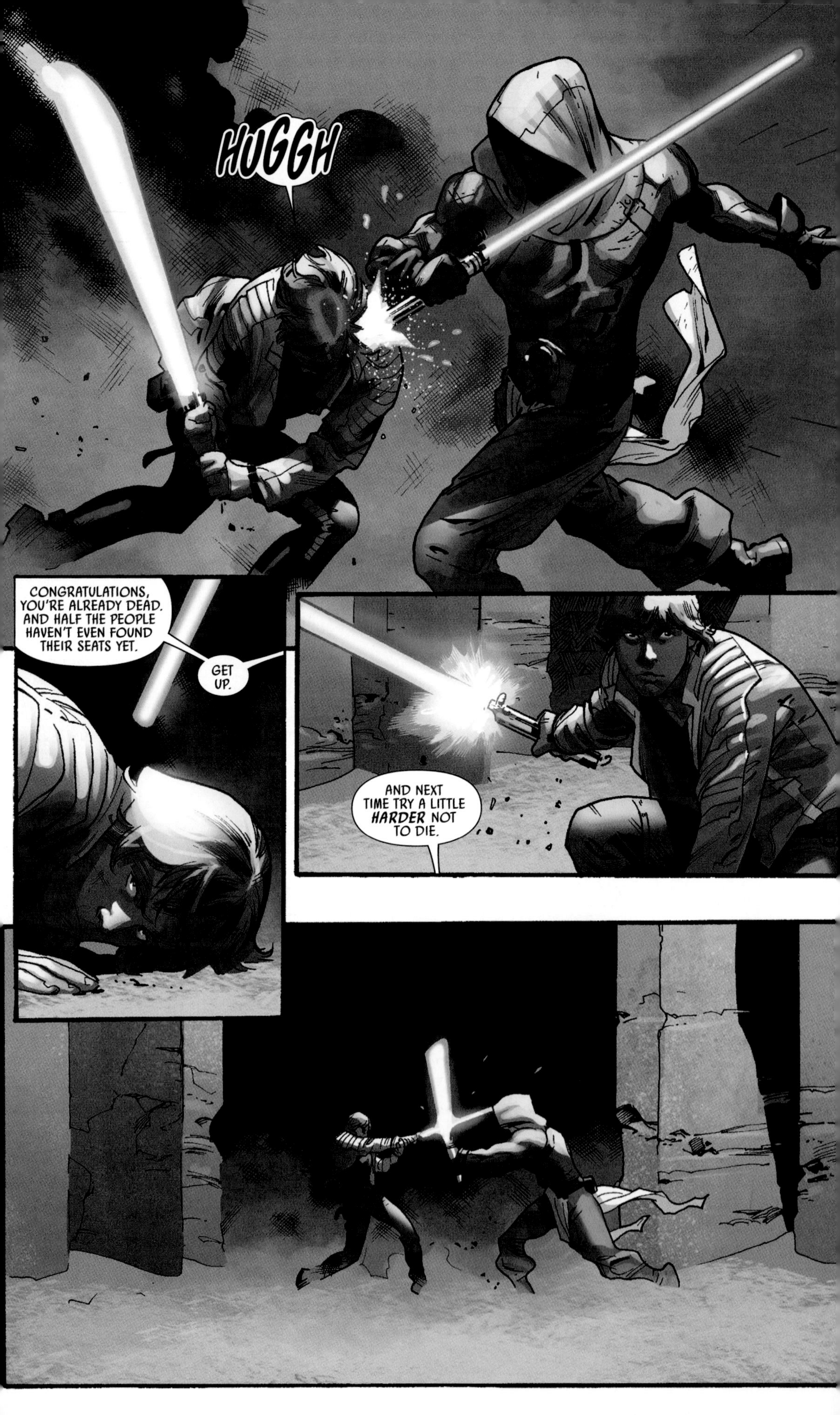
HUGGH
CONGRATULATIONS, YOU'RE ALREADY DEAD. AND HALF THE PEOPLE HAVEN'T EVEN FOUND THEIR SEATS YET.
GET UP.
AND NEXT TIME TRY A LITTLE HARDER NOT TO DIE.

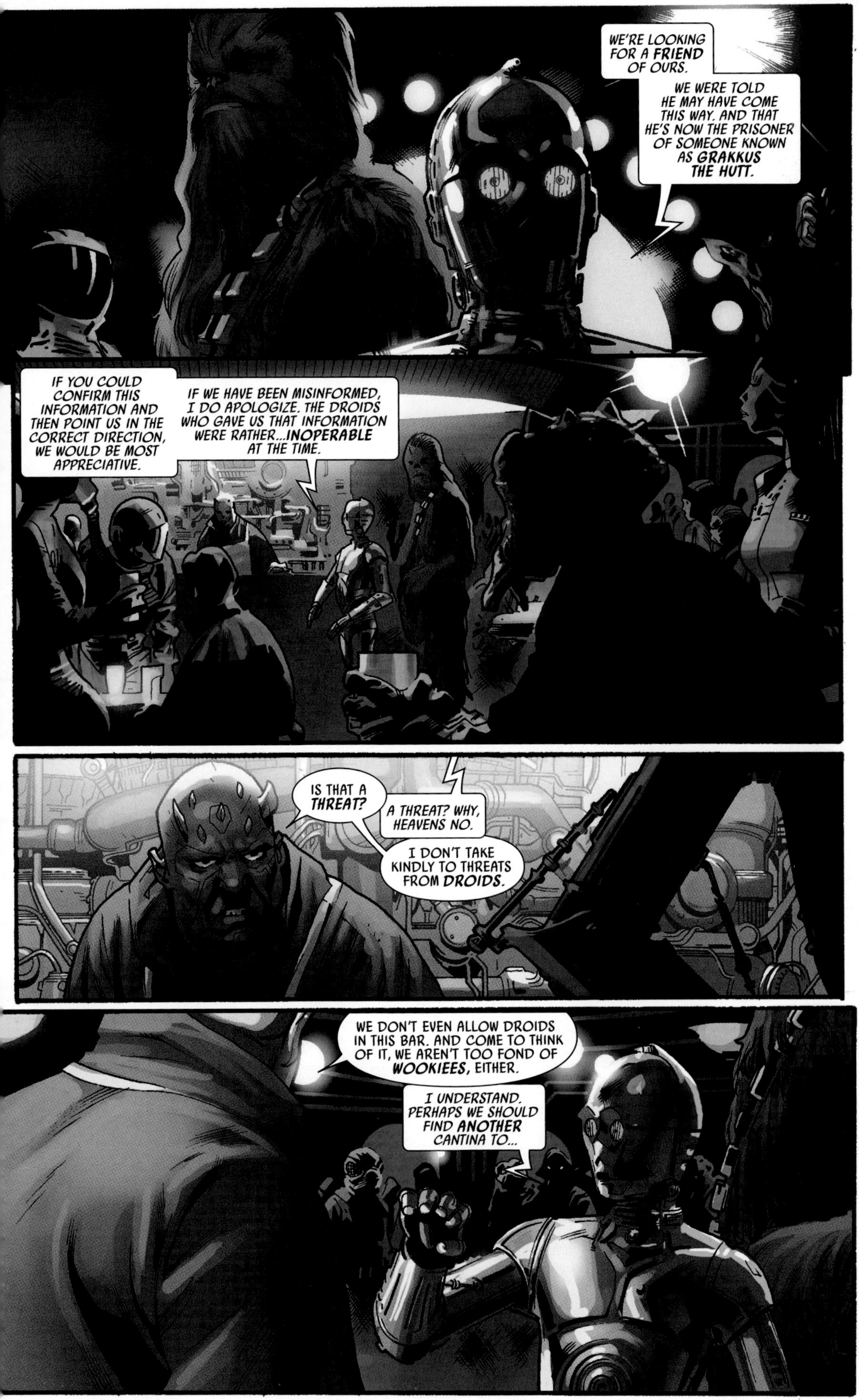

WE'RE LOOKING FOR A FRIEND OF OURS.
WE WERE TOLD HE MAY HAVE COME THIS WAY. AND THAT HE'S NOW THE PRISONER OF SOMEONE KNOWN AS GRAKKUS THE HUTT.
IF YOU COULD CONFIRM THIS INFORMATION AND THEN POINT US IN THE CORRECT DIRECTION, WE WOULD BE MOST APPRECIATIVE.
IF WE HAVE BEEN MISINFORMED, I DO APOLOGIZE. THE DROIDS WHO GAVE US THAT INFORMATION WERE RATHER...INOPERABLE AT THE TIME.
IS THAT A THREAT?
A THREAT? WHY, HEAVENS NO.
I DON'T TAKE KINDLY TO THREATS FROM DROIDS.
WE DON'T EVEN ALLOW DROIDS IN THIS BAR. AND COME TO THINK OF IT, WE AREN'T TOO FOND OF WOOKIEES, EITHER.
I UNDERSTAND. PERHAPS WE SHOULD FIND ANOTHER CANTINA TO...

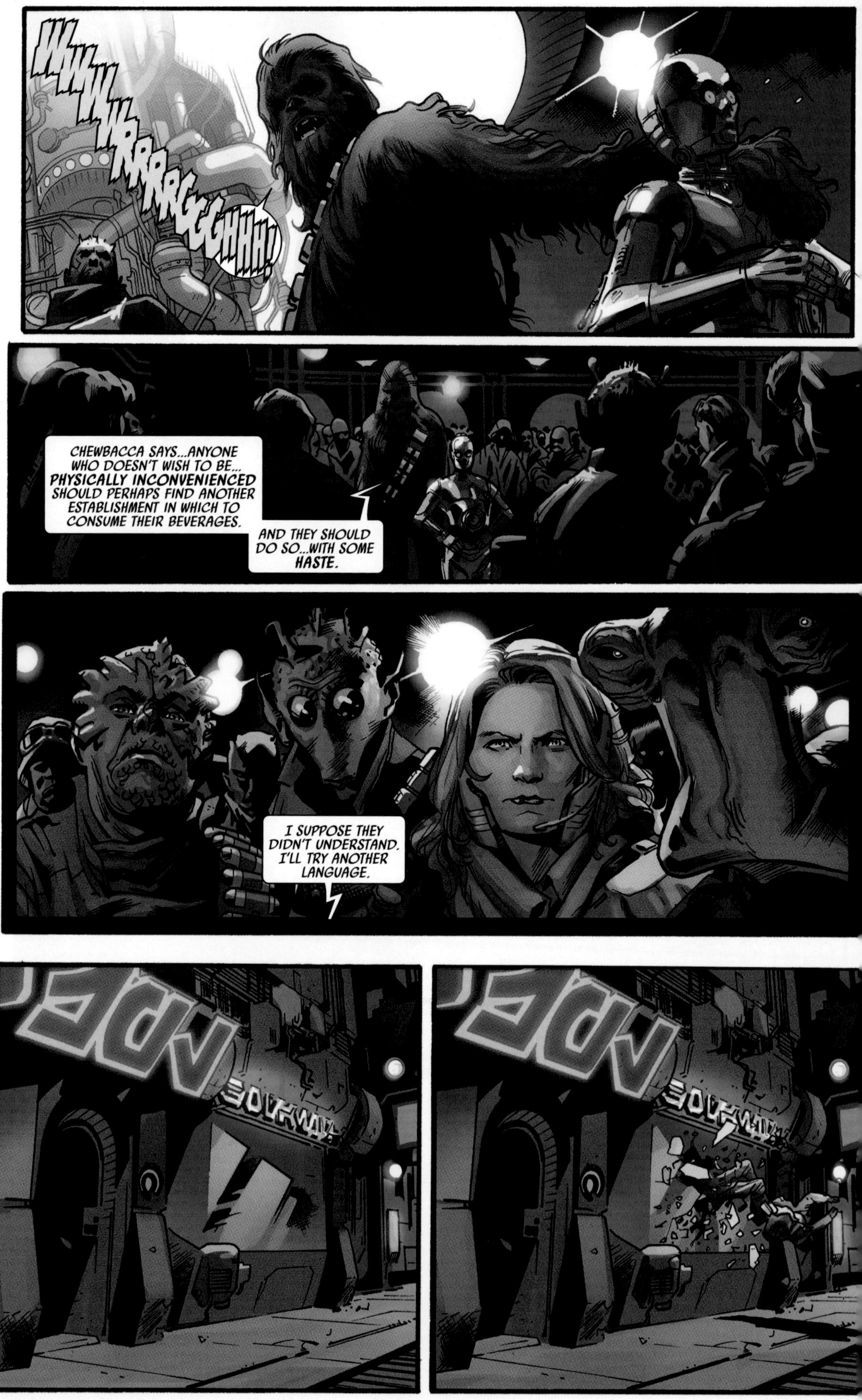
WWWWRRRRRGGGHHHH!!
CHEWBACCA SAYS...ANYONE WHO DOESN'T WISH TO BE... PHYSICALLY INCONVENIENCED SHOULD PERHAPS FIND ANOTHER ESTABLISHMENT IN WHICH TO CONSUME THEIR BEVERAGES.
AND THEY SHOULD DO SO...WITH SOME HASTE.
I SUPPOSE THEY DIDN'T UNDERSTAND. I'LL TRY ANOTHER LANGUAGE.

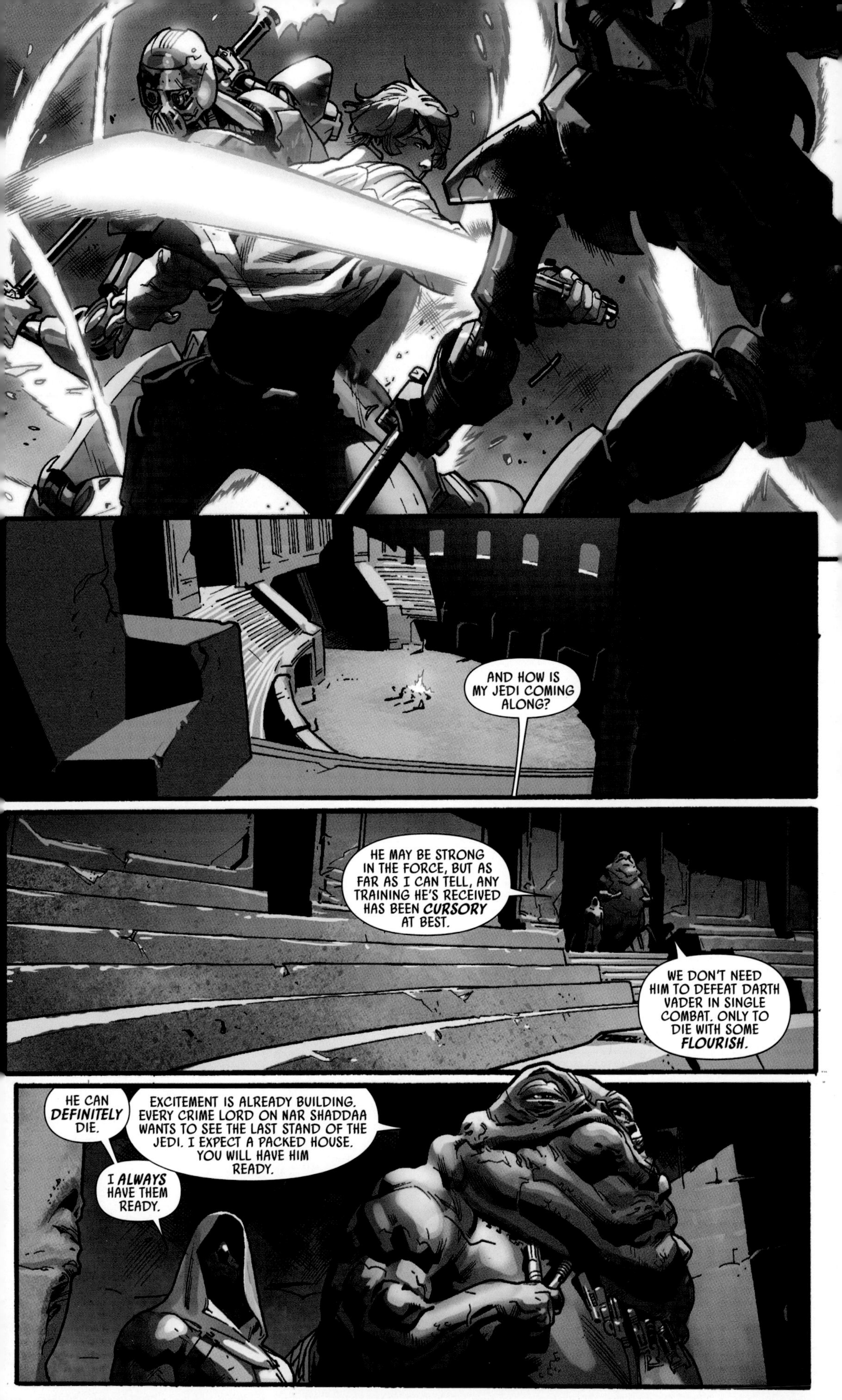
AND HOW IS MY JEDI COMING ALONG?
HE MAY BE STRONG IN THE FORCE, BUT AS FAR AS I CAN TELL, ANY TRAINING HE'S RECEIVED HAS BEEN *CURSORY* AT BEST.
WE DON'T NEED HIM TO DEFEAT DARTH VADER IN SINGLE COMBAT. ONLY TO DIE WITH SOME *FLOURISH*.
HE CAN *DEFINITELY* DIE.
I *ALWAYS* HAVE THEM READY.
EXCITEMENT IS ALREADY BUILDING. EVERY CRIME LORD ON NAR SHADDAA WANTS TO SEE THE LAST STAND OF THE JEDI. I EXPECT A PACKED HOUSE. YOU WILL HAVE HIM READY.

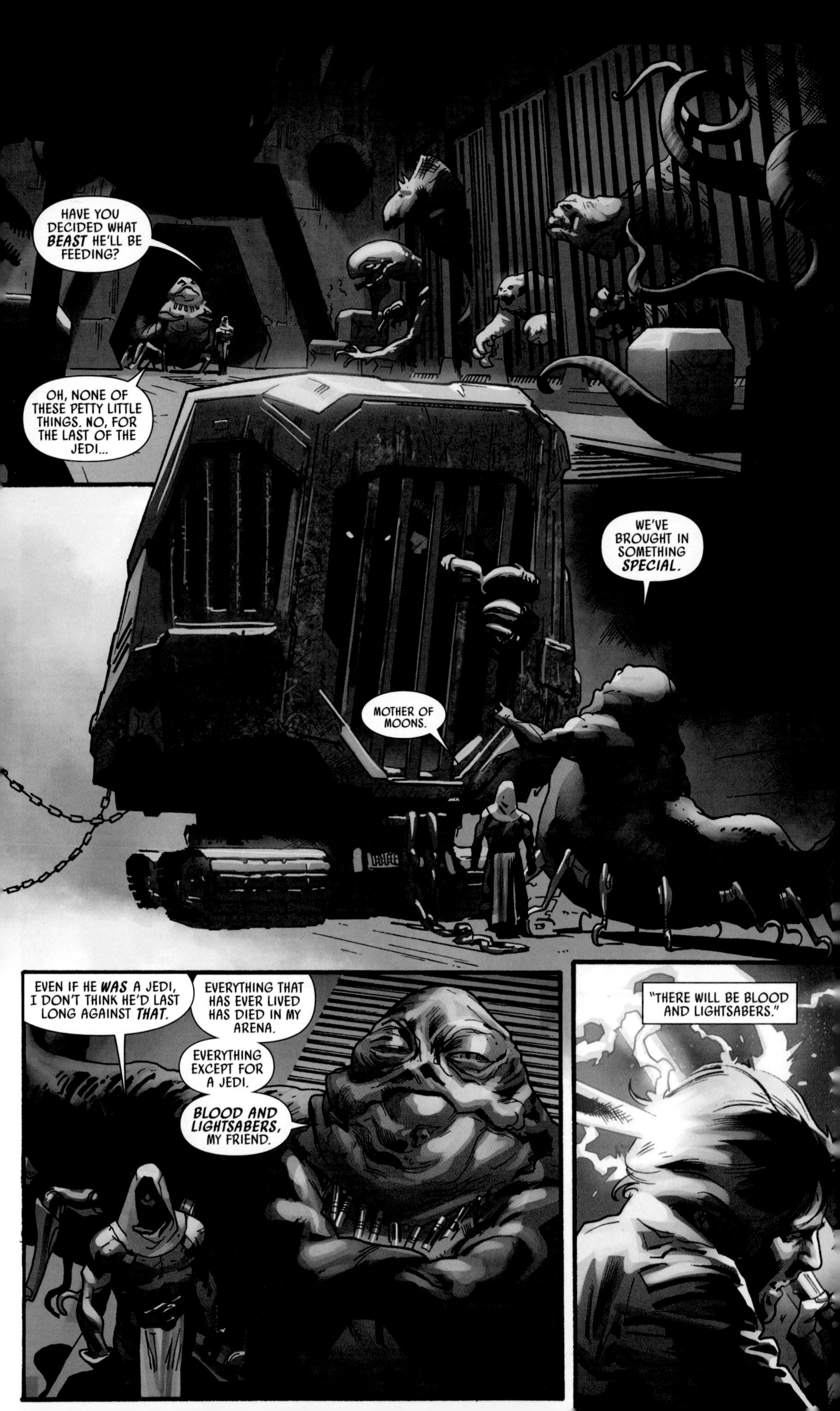
HAVE YOU DECIDED WHAT BEAST HE'LL BE FEEDING?
OH, NONE OF THESE PETTY LITTLE THINGS. NO, FOR THE LAST OF THE JEDI...
WE'VE BROUGHT IN SOMETHING SPECIAL.
MOTHER OF MOONS.
EVEN IF HE WAS A JEDI, I DON'T THINK HE'D LAST LONG AGAINST THAT.
EVERYTHING THAT HAS EVER LIVED HAS DIED IN MY ARENA.
EVERYTHING EXCEPT FOR A JEDI.
BLOOD AND LIGHTSABERS, MY FRIEND.
"THERE WILL BE BLOOD AND LIGHTSABERS."

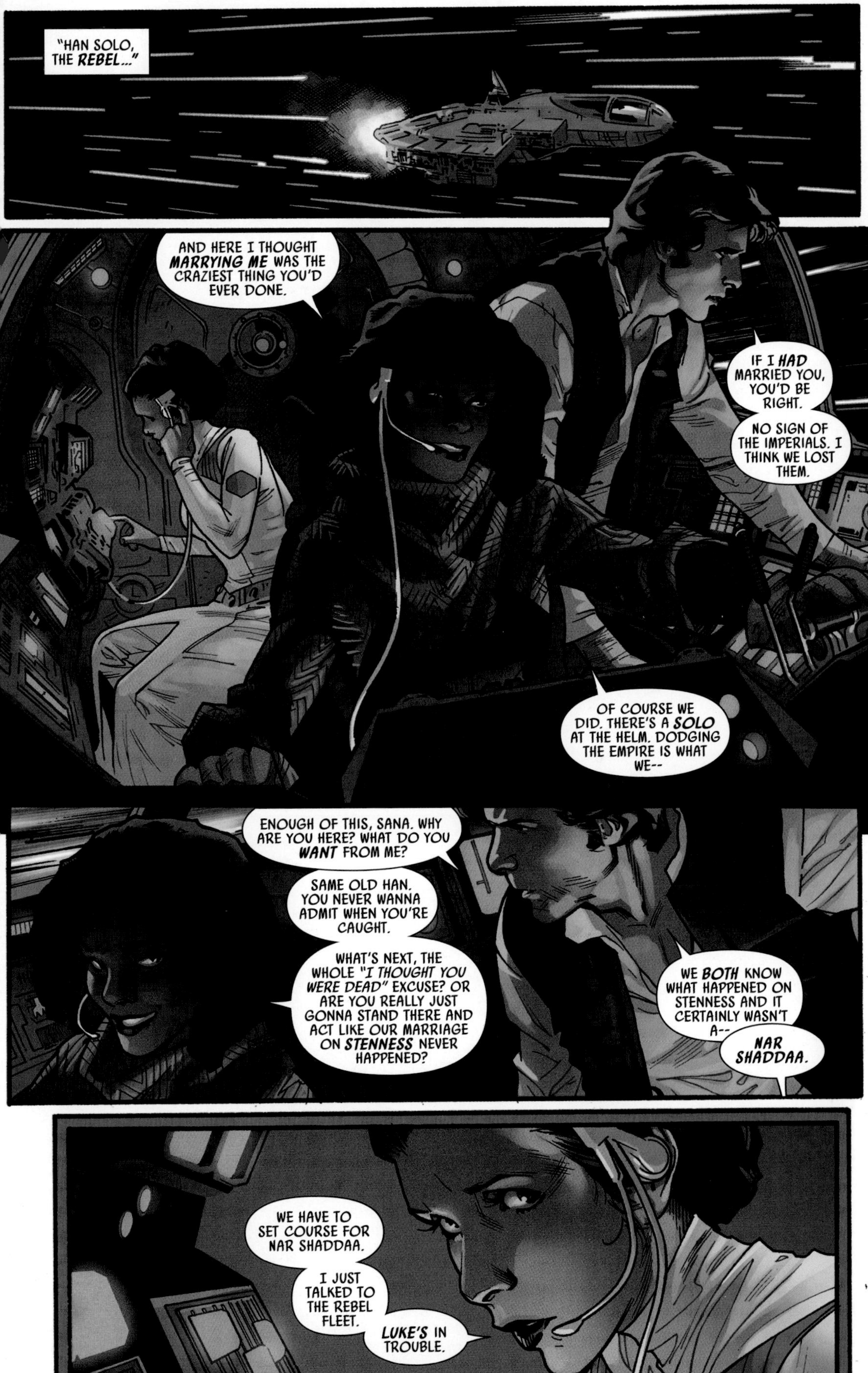

"HAN SOLO, THE REBEL..."
AND HERE I THOUGHT MARRYING ME WAS THE CRAZIEST THING YOU'D EVER DONE.
IF I HAD MARRIED YOU, YOU'D BE RIGHT.
NO SIGN OF THE IMPERIALS. I THINK WE LOST THEM.
OF COURSE WE DID. THERE'S A SOLO AT THE HELM. DODGING THE EMPIRE IS WHAT WE--
ENOUGH OF THIS, SANA. WHY ARE YOU HERE? WHAT DO YOU WANT FROM ME?
SAME OLD HAN. YOU NEVER WANNA ADMIT WHEN YOU'RE CAUGHT.
WHAT'S NEXT, THE WHOLE "I THOUGHT YOU WERE DEAD" EXCUSE? OR ARE YOU REALLY JUST GONNA STAND THERE AND ACT LIKE OUR MARRIAGE ON STENNESS NEVER HAPPENED?
WE BOTH KNOW WHAT HAPPENED ON STENNESS AND IT CERTAINLY WASN'T A--
NAR SHADDAA.
WE HAVE TO SET COURSE FOR NAR SHADDAA.
I JUST TALKED TO THE REBEL FLEET.
LUKE'S IN TROUBLE.

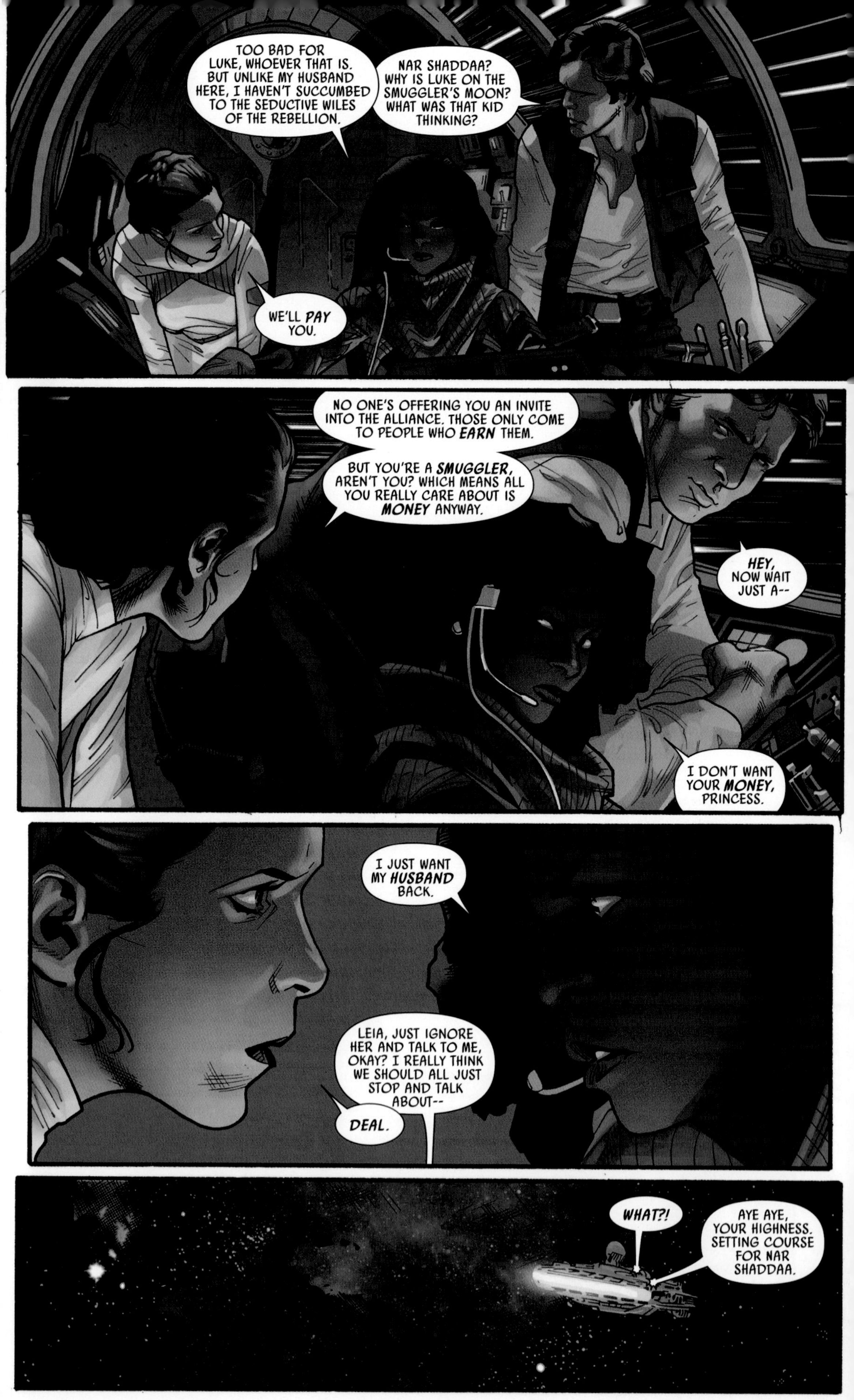

TOO BAD FOR LUKE, WHOEVER THAT IS. BUT UNLIKE MY HUSBAND HERE, I HAVEN'T SUCCUMBED TO THE SEDUCTIVE WILES OF THE REBELLION.
NAR SHADDAA? WHY IS LUKE ON THE SMUGGLER'S MOON? WHAT WAS THAT KID THINKING?
WE'LL PAY YOU.
NO ONE'S OFFERING YOU AN INVITE INTO THE ALLIANCE. THOSE ONLY COME TO PEOPLE WHO EARN THEM.
BUT YOU'RE A SMUGGLER, AREN'T YOU? WHICH MEANS ALL YOU REALLY CARE ABOUT IS MONEY ANYWAY.
HEY, NOW WAIT JUST A--
I DON'T WANT YOUR MONEY, PRINCESS.
I JUST WANT MY HUSBAND BACK.
LEIA, JUST IGNORE HER AND TALK TO ME, OKAY? I REALLY THINK WE SHOULD ALL JUST STOP AND TALK ABOUT--
DEAL.
WHAT?!
AYE AYE, YOUR HIGHNESS. SETTING COURSE FOR NAR SHADDAA.

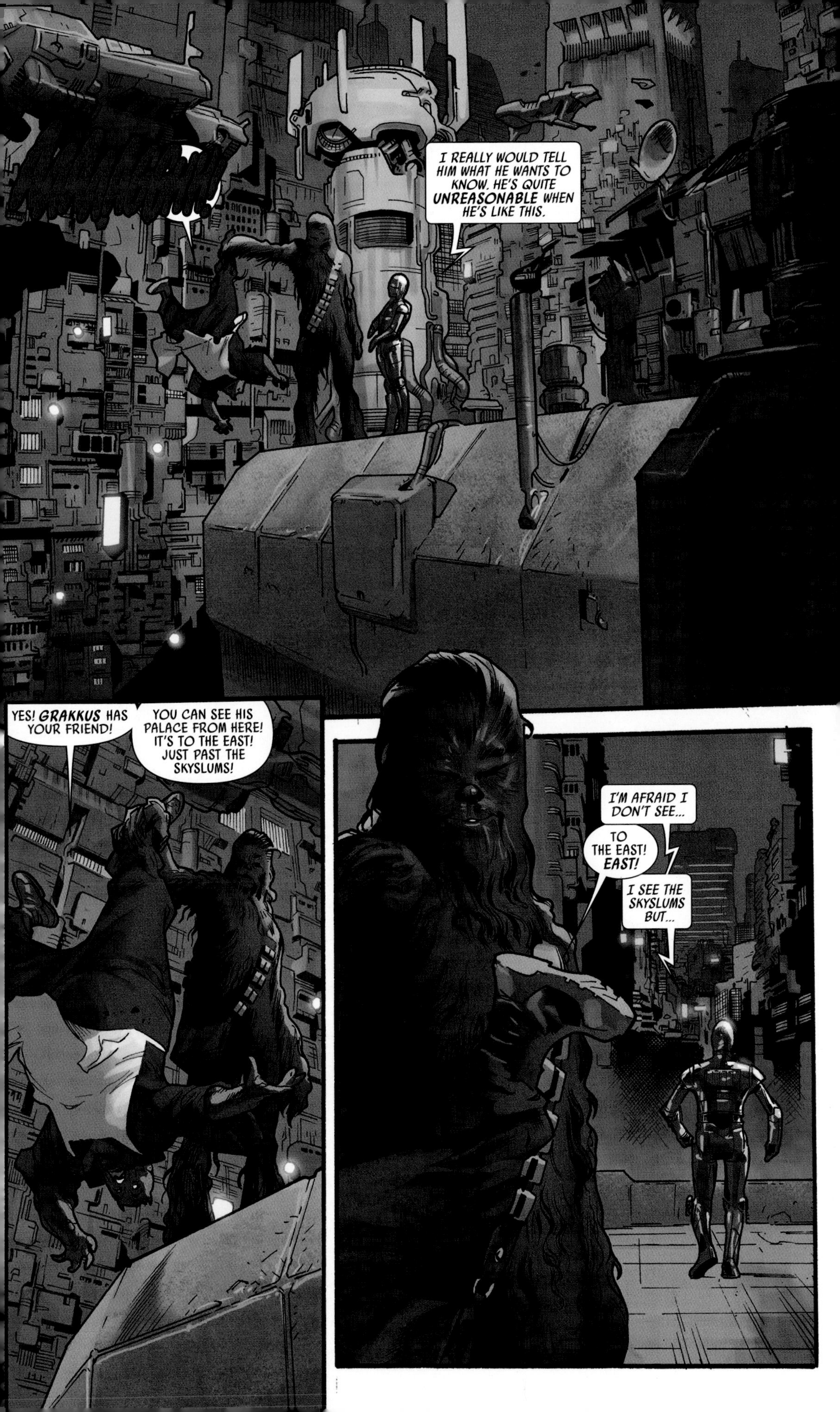
I REALLY WOULD TELL HIM WHAT HE WANTS TO KNOW. HE'S QUITE UNREASONABLE WHEN HE'S LIKE THIS.
YES! GRAKKUS HAS YOUR FRIEND!
YOU CAN SEE HIS PALACE FROM HERE! IT'S TO THE EAST! JUST PAST THE SKYSLUMS!
I'M AFRAID I DON'T SEE...
TO THE EAST! EAST!
I SEE THE SKYSLUMS BUT...

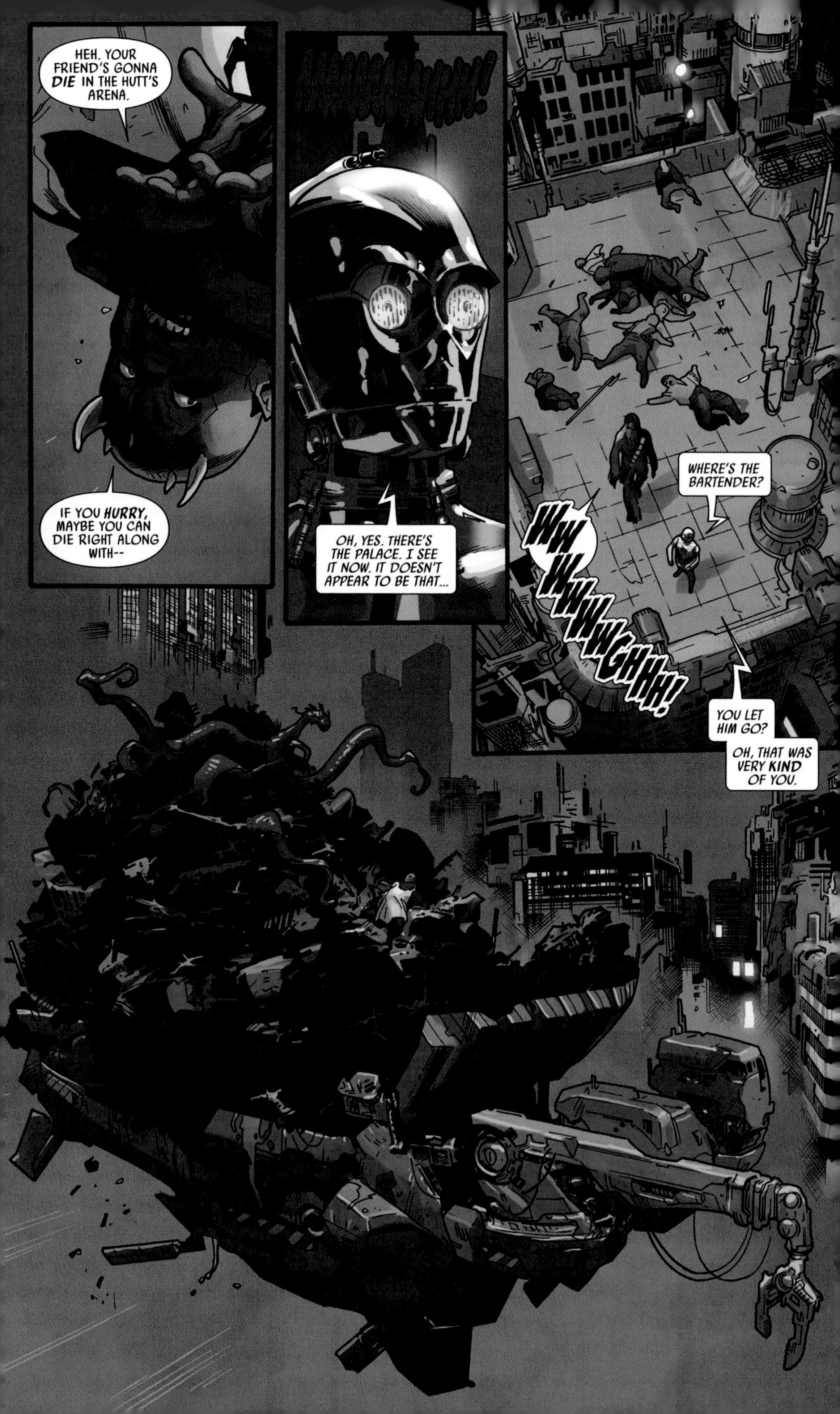
HEH. YOUR FRIEND'S GONNA DIE IN THE HUTT'S ARENA.
IF YOU HURRY, MAYBE YOU CAN DIE RIGHT ALONG WITH--
OH, YES. THERE'S THE PALACE. I SEE IT NOW. IT DOESN'T APPEAR TO BE THAT...
WHERE'S THE BARTENDER?
WWWWWWWGHHH!
YOU LET HIM GO?
OH, THAT WAS VERY KIND OF YOU.

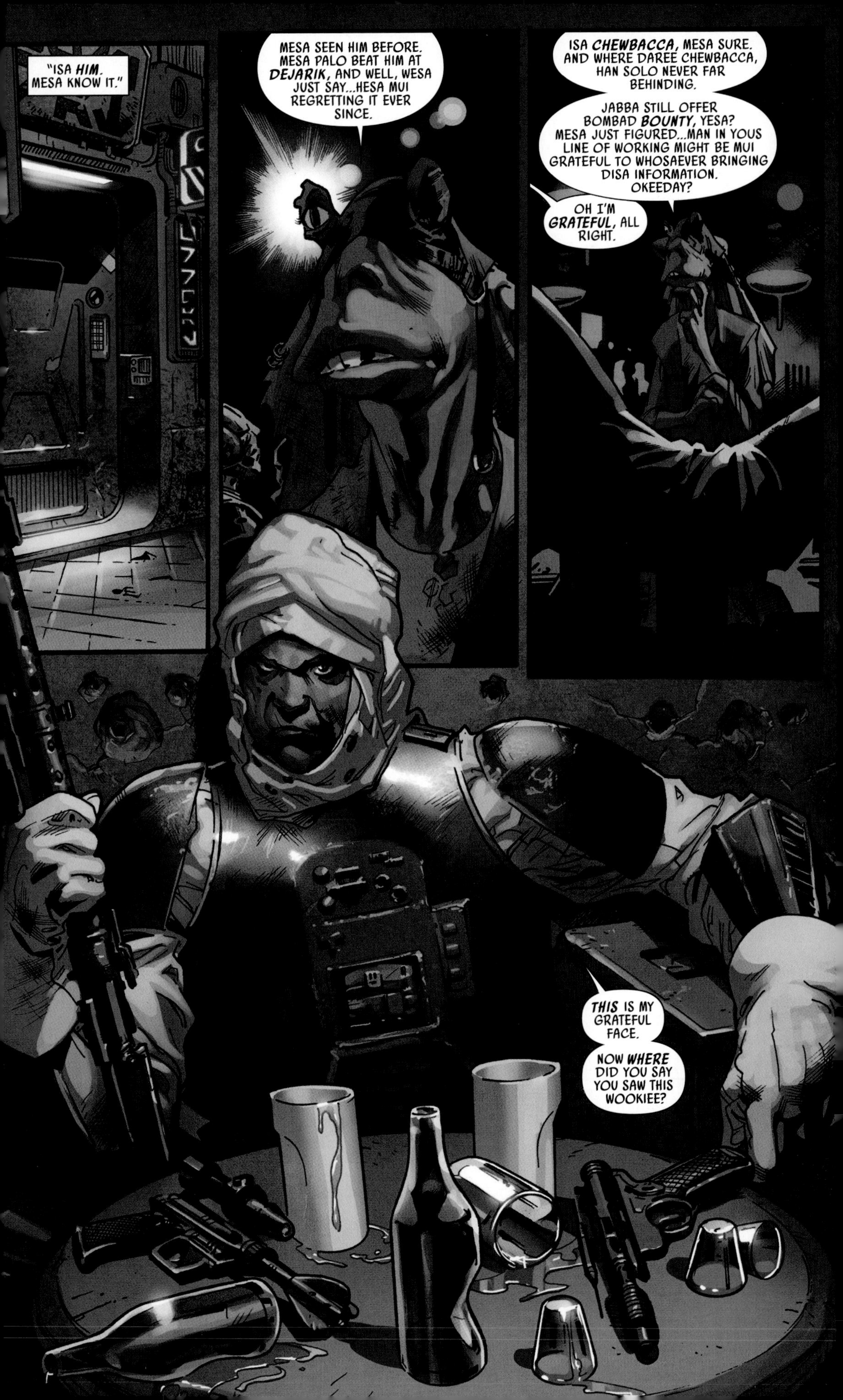
"ISA HIM. MESA KNOW IT."
MESA SEEN HIM BEFORE. MESA PALO BEAT HIM AT DEJARIK, AND WELL, WESA JUST SAY...HESA MUI REGRETTING IT EVER SINCE.
ISA CHEWBACCA, MESA SURE. AND WHERE DAREE CHEWBACCA, HAN SOLO NEVER FAR BEHINDING.
JABBA STILL OFFER BOMBAD BOUNTY, YESA? MESA JUST FIGURED...MAN IN YOUS LINE OF WORKING MIGHT BE MUI GRATEFUL TO WHOSAEVER BRINGING DISA INFORMATION. OKEEDAY?
OH I'M GRATEFUL, ALL RIGHT.
THIS IS MY GRATEFUL FACE.
NOW WHERE DID YOU SAY YOU SAW THIS WOOKIEE?

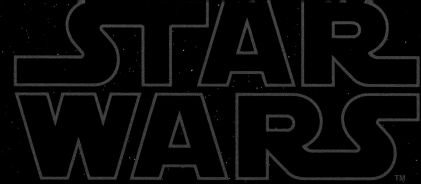

STAR WARS

SHOWDOWN ON THE SMUGGLER'S MOON

COLLECT THEM ALL!

Set of 6 Hardcover Books ISBN: 978-1-61479-553-7

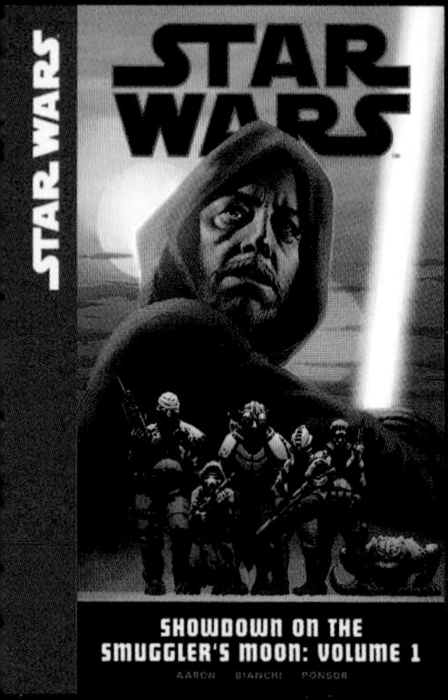
STAR WARS
STAR WARS
SHOWDOWN ON THE SMUGGLER'S MOON: VOLUME 1
AARON BIANCHI PONSOR

Hardcover Book ISBN
978-1-61479-554-4

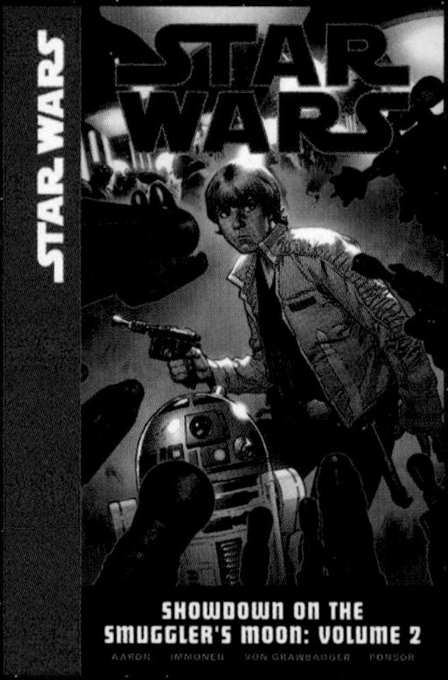
STAR WARS
STAR WARS
SHOWDOWN ON THE SMUGGLER'S MOON: VOLUME 2
AARON IMMONEN VON GRAWBADGER PONSOR

Hardcover Book ISBN
978-1-61479-555-1

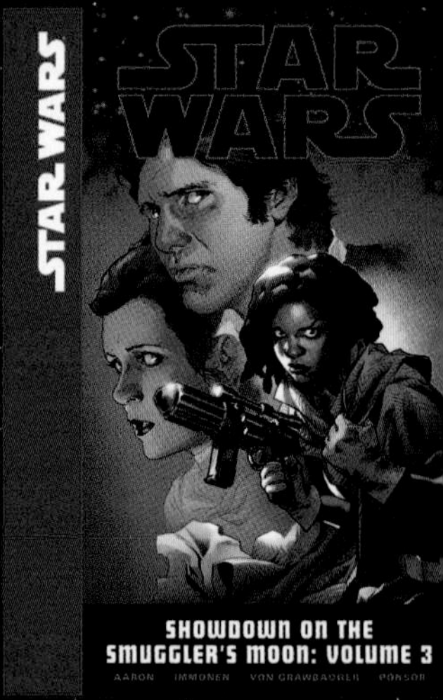
STAR WARS
STAR WARS
SHOWDOWN ON THE SMUGGLER'S MOON: VOLUME 3
AARON IMMONEN VON GRAWBADGER PONSOR

Hardcover Book ISBN
978-1-61479-556-8

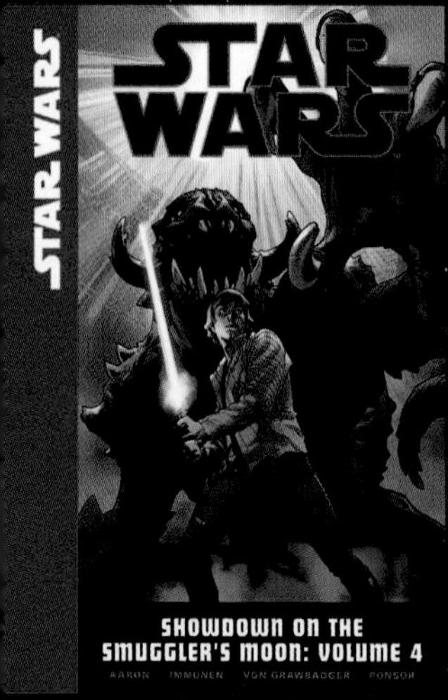
STAR WARS
STAR WARS
SHOWDOWN ON THE SMUGGLER'S MOON: VOLUME 4
AARON IMMONEN VON GRAWBADGER PONSOR

Hardcover Book ISBN
978-1-61479-557-5

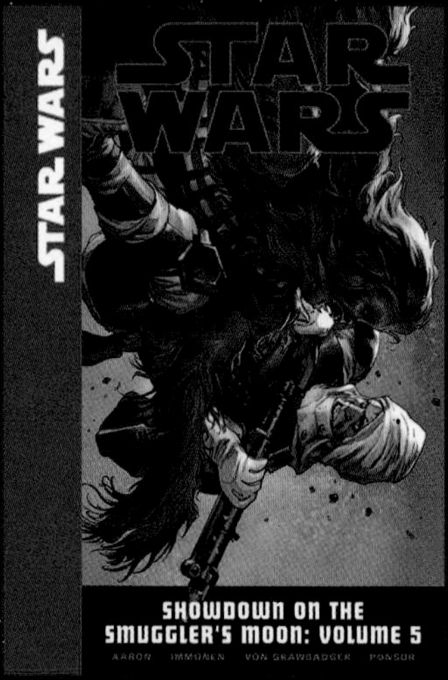
STAR WARS
STAR WARS
SHOWDOWN ON THE SMUGGLER'S MOON: VOLUME 5
AARON IMMONEN VON GRAWBADGER PONSOR

Hardcover Book ISBN
978-1-61479-558-2

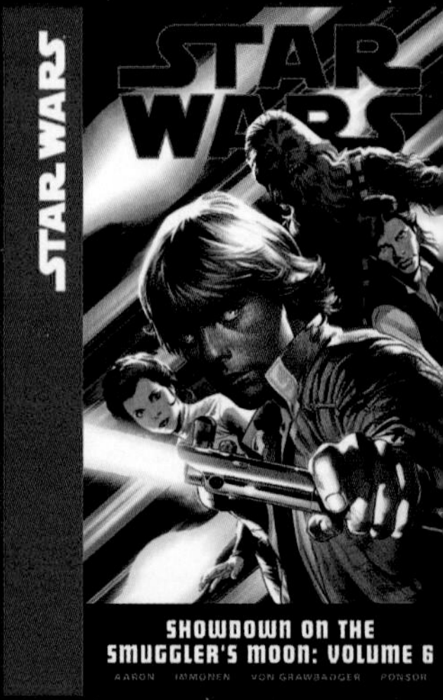
STAR WARS
STAR WARS
SHOWDOWN ON THE SMUGGLER'S MOON: VOLUME 6
AARON IMMONEN VON GRAWBADGER PONSOR

Hardcover Book ISBN
978-1-61479-559-9